For my husband, Dustin.
Thank you for your love and support.

Published by Circle Time Books, 2022

Edited by Sam Cabbage & Rob Daniel
Printed in the USA
Hardcover: ISBN: 978-1-7342952-4-5
Paperback: ISBN: 978-1-7342952-3-8

Cardboard Rosie

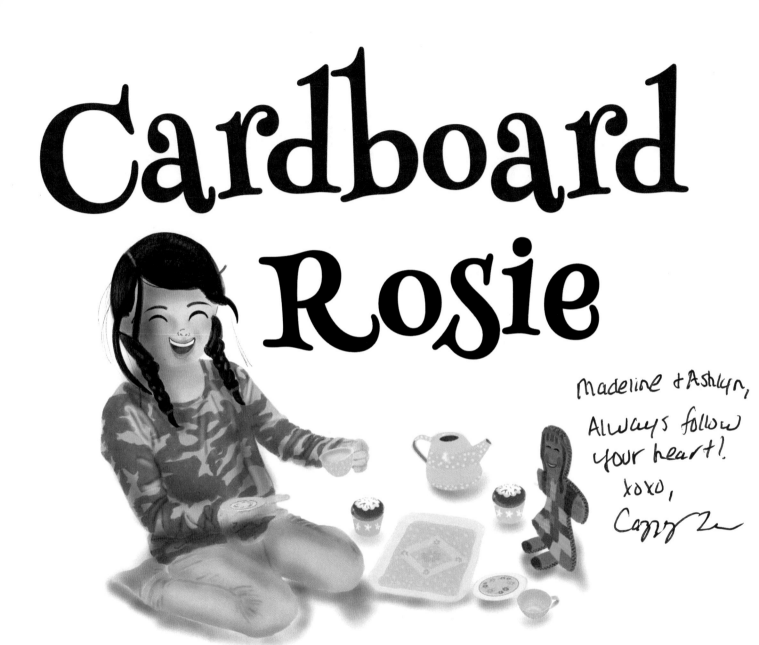

Madeline & Ashlyn,

Always follow your heart!.

xoxo,

Cazzy

Written & Illustrated by
Cazzy Zahursky

Emma loved her daddy, but the only time she got to see him was
when he tucked her in at bedtime.

Every night Emma's daddy sang to her, "You're my special girl, I wouldn't change you for the world. I love you to the Milky Way and Mars, together we will see the stars. Good night, Pumpkin."

Every morning at breakfast, Daddy asked, "What do you want for your birthday, Pumpkin?"

And every morning she replied, "A Forever Doll!" Emma wanted a Forever Doll so badly, it hurt.

"We don't have a lot of money right now, but I will try my hardest." Looking down at Emma's big brown eyes, Daddy said, "I promise, I'll take good care of you, Pumpkin."

Emma's eyes twinkled with hope because Daddy always kept his promises.

One Saturday morning, Daddy said, "I have a surprise for you!"
Emma smiled from ear to ear. She had been waiting *forever* for this moment.
"A Forever Doll!"

Staring at the cracks in his callused hands, Daddy said, "No, Pumpkin, it's not. But, I have some time before work tonight, so I was thinking we could spend the whole afternoon together. Just me and you."

Nervously, he glanced down at Emma and added, "We could make our own Forever Doll." Emma forced the corners of her mouth to curl up, just enough to look like a smile. She didn't want Daddy to see her disappointment.

That afternoon they drew and cut together, they played together, they told stories together, and they laughed together.

"Ta-da! Your very own Forever Doll," exclaimed Daddy. Emma giggled.
"I'm sorry it's not a real Forever Doll."

It wasn't even close, but Emma looked up at Daddy and smiled anyway.

After that Daddy worked more and more, and Emma saw him less and less. Each night she waited for him to come home and tuck her in. One night it felt like he would never come.

She noticed the cardboard doll on her nightstand, picked her up and said,
"I will call you Rosie."

Emma played with Rosie. Emma laughed with Rosie. Emma cried with Rosie. Emma got excited with Rosie. Emma felt scared with Rosie.

Emma did everything with Rosie.

Every day Emma took Rosie with her to school. One day Rosie slipped out of Emma's backpack and floated onto the floor. A classmate grabbed Rosie, "What is this?"
"It's Rosie."
"Why does it look like a Forever Doll?"
"Give her back."
"Here's your cardboard doll. I have a real one anyway."

Emma looked at Rosie and said, "Don't worry, I promise I'll always take good care of you, Pumpkin."

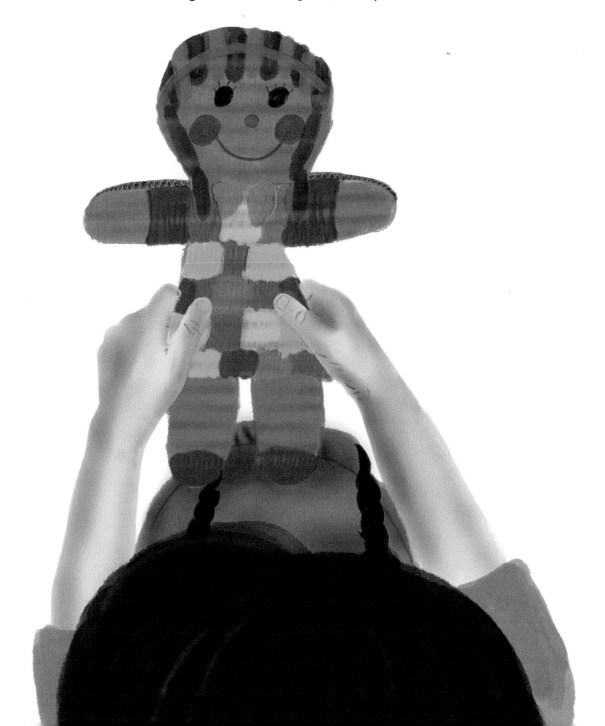

One morning at breakfast, Emma asked Mommy, "Where's Daddy?"
"He had to start work early today, sweetie. He will be back to tuck you in tonight."
Emma hugged Rosie extra tight. As she did, she noticed a dirty spot on Rosie's dress.

Emma tenderly told Rosie, "I'll clean it, Pumpkin."

So Emma grabbed a stool from under a table, dragged it across the bathroom and climbed up to reach the sink.

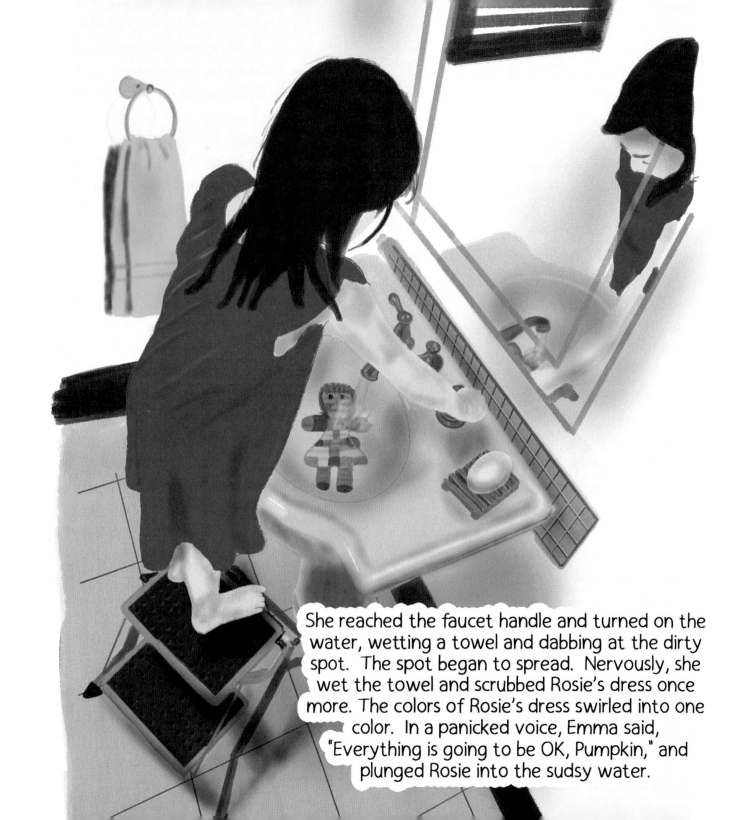

She reached the faucet handle and turned on the water, wetting a towel and dabbing at the dirty spot. The spot began to spread. Nervously, she wet the towel and scrubbed Rosie's dress once more. The colors of Rosie's dress swirled into one color. In a panicked voice, Emma said, "Everything is going to be OK, Pumpkin," and plunged Rosie into the sudsy water.

Rosie's smile faded and her eyes washed away. Emma quickly reached for what was left of Rosie, and her world seemed to stop.

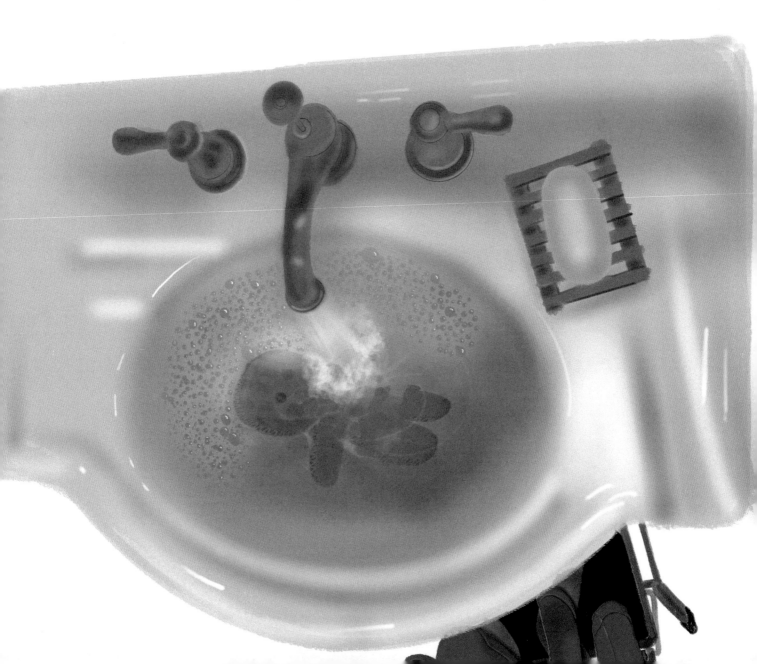

At bedtime, Emma heard Daddy coming into her room.

"Mommy told me what happened to Rosie today."

Hundreds of thoughts whirled through Emma's head. She tried hard to hold back the tears. Emma threw herself onto her pillow and cried, "It's not fair."

Daddy leaned in and said, "It's OK to feel mad. Do you want to talk about it?"

Daddy felt he had let Emma down. He had not been able to buy her a real Forever Doll when she asked for one, and now Rosie was ruined. He wished he could take her pain away. "I'm here for you, if you need me."

Emma couldn't stop thinking about Rosie. She remembered the morning at school when she realized how important Rosie was to her. She remembered singing to Rosie as she waited for Daddy to come home. Who was she going to sing to now? Would bedtime ever be the same again?

Then she remembered Daddy. It was Daddy who sang *her* that song. She remembered it was *Daddy* who made Rosie for *her*.

Daddy gently reached out to pat Emma's back, "I'm so sorry Pumpkin."
Tears poured down Emma's cheeks and sobs shook her little body.
"You miss Rosie a lot, don't you?"
"I'm not crying because I miss Rosie."
Daddy was confused, "Then why are you crying?"

Daddy opened his arms wide and embraced Emma like a doll and sang to her, "You're my special girl, I wouldn't change you for the world. I love you to the Milky Way and Mars, together we will see the stars."

Emma felt the stubble on Daddy's face. At that moment, they needed nothing more to make them happy.

Daddy whispered, "Well, I have some time right now..."

They both glanced at a cardboard box sitting in the corner, and smiled.

ABOUT THE AUTHOR AND ILLUSTRATOR

Cazzy Zahursky is a wife and mother of two girls and a dog. She enjoys spending time with her family, reading, traveling, volunteering at her children's schools, and working out. She stays busy and inspired by her girls on a daily basis. She loves teaching them lessons through storytelling. Whether she's playing around with her girls or exploring new hiking trails, she enjoys every memorable moment.

Made in the USA
Middletown, DE
13 June 2022